BEATRIX POTTER

Children's Classics

BEATRIX POTTER

THE TALE OF a FIERCE BAD RABBIT

Children's **Classics**

SOVEREIGN

LONDON · NEW YORK · TORONTO · SAO PAULO · MOSCOW
PARIS · MADRID · BERLIN · ROME · MEXICO CITY · MUMBAI · SEOUL · DOHA
TOKYO · SYDNEY · CAPE TOWN · AUCKLAND · BEIJING

New Edition, Children's Classics

Published by Sovereign Classic

This Edition
First published in 2018

ISBN: 9781787246331

CONTENTS

THE TALE OF A FIERCE BAD RABBIT   7

THE TALE OF A FIERCE BAD RABBIT

This is a fierce bad Rabbit; look at his savage
whiskers, and his claws and his turned-up tail.

This is a nice gentle Rabbit. His mother has given him a carrot.

The bad Rabbit would like some carrot.

He doesn't say "Please." He takes it!

And he scratches the good Rabbit very badly.

The good Rabbit creeps away, and hides in a hole. It feels sad.

This is a man with a gun.

He sees something sitting on a bench. He
thinks it is a very funny bird!

He comes creeping up behind the trees.

And then he shoots—Bang!

This is what happens—

But this is all he finds on the bench, when he rushes up with his gun.

The good Rabbit peeps out of its hole,

And it sees the bad Rabbit tearing past—
without any tail or whiskers!

THE END